EVERYDAY MINDFULNESS
Breath by Breath

Published in North America by Free Spirit Publishing Inc., Minneapolis, Minnesota, 2018

Library of Congress Cataloging-in-Publication Data
Names: Christelis, Paul, author. | Paganelli, Elisa, 1985– illustrator.
Title: Breath by breath : a mindfulness guide to feeling calm / written by Paul Christelis ; illustrated by Elisa Paganelli.
Description: Minneapolis, Minnesota : Free Spirit Publishing, 2018. | Series: Everyday mindfulness
Identifiers: LCCN 2017060596 | ISBN 9781631983313 (hardcover) | ISBN 1631983318 (hardcover)
Subjects: LCSH: Breathing exercises—Juvenile literature. | Calmness—Juvenile literature.
Classification: LCC RA782 .C497 2018 | DDC 613/.192—dc23 LC record available at https://lccn.loc.gov/2017060596

Reading Level Grade 2; Interest Level Ages 5–9; Fountas & Pinnell Guided Reading Level L

10 9 8 7 6 5 4 3 2 1
Printed in China
H13660518

Free Spirit Publishing Inc.
6325 Sandburg Road, Suite 100
Minneapolis, MN 55427-3674
(612) 338-2068
help4kids@freespirit.com
www.freespirit.com

First published in 2018 by Franklin Watts, a division of Hachette Children's Books • London, UK, and Sydney, Australia

Copyright © The Watts Publishing Group, 2018

The rights of Paul Christelis to be identified as the author and Elisa Paganelli as the illustrator of this Work have been asserted in accordance with the Copyright, Designs and Patents Act, 1988.

Managing editor: Victoria Brooker
Creative design: Lisa Peacock

Breath by Breath

A MINDFULNESS GUIDE TO FEELING CALM

Written by
Paul Christelis

Illustrated by
Elisa Paganelli

free spirit
PUBLISHING®

WHAT IS MINDFULNESS?

Mindfulness is a way of paying attention to our present-moment experience with an attitude of kindness and curiosity. Most of the time, our attention is distracted—often by thoughts about the past or future—and this can make us feel jumpy, worried, self-critical, and confused.

By gently moving our focus from our busy minds and into the present moment, we begin to let go of distraction and learn to tap into an ever-present supply of well-being and ease that resides in the here and now. Mindfulness can also help us improve concentration, calm unpleasant emotions, and even boost our immune systems.

In this book, children are encouraged to develop mindfulness by using their breathing as an "object" to pay attention to. Breathing happens naturally, in the present moment, and simply noticing the sensations of the breath can bring a sense of peace and calm.

Readers are also invited to gratefully acknowledge the gift of life bestowed by each breath. Cultivating this attitude of gratitude helps us experience life as wondrous and special, even in times of difficulty.

The book can be read interactively, allowing readers to pause at various points and turn their attention to how they are feeling or what they are noticing. Watch for the **PAUSE BUTTON** in the text. It suggests opportunities to encourage readers to be curious about what they observe, such as the texture or temperature of their breath. Each time this **PAUSE BUTTON** is used, mindfulness is deepened.

Try not to rush this pause. Really allow enough time for children to stay with their experience. It doesn't matter if what they feel or notice is pleasant or unpleasant. What's important is to pay attention to it with a friendly attitude. This will introduce them to a way of being in the world that promotes calmness, health, and happiness.

This is the story of three different children who have one very important thing in common. In fact, they also have something in common with you! Yes, the you who is reading this book right now.

Do you have any idea what Sam, Lenny, Rosa, and you all share? Here's a clue: It can't be seen and, unless you are exercising, it probably can't be heard. But if you are very still, close your eyes, and concentrate on what's happening in your body, you will **feel** it.

👆 PAUSE BUTTON

Try it now! Close your eyes and see if you can notice what's happening in your body. Can you feel something?

Aha! What we all share is **breath!** Without it, we wouldn't be alive, so it's very important indeed. But we hardly notice that we are breathing unless we are out of breath or feeling sick.

For Sam, it doesn't matter if he is feeling well or feeling sick. Every day he spends a few minutes noticing his breathing. He does this each morning, sitting up in bed. Noticing his breath helps him feel calm and relaxed. It's a great way to start the day!

You might wonder, "How can I notice *my* breathing?" It's easy! All you need to do is sit up straight, let your body relax, and close your eyes. Imagine that you are a cat sitting perfectly still, or maybe a tree—upright and strong.

Now, see if you can feel the air moving into your nose as you breathe in, and feel the air moving out of your nose as you breathe out. Just let breathing happen as it usually does, without trying to breathe in a special way.

Take a minute to feel your breath moving in and out of your nose. You can also feel the breath moving in your belly. Try placing your hand on your belly and feel it moving up and down as you breathe for another minute.

Maybe, like Sam, you noticed that your mind can be quite busy while you're focusing attention on your breath. You can get lost in thoughts, memories, or **worries**.

If that happens, try silently counting your breaths. Every in-breath and out-breath is counted as one full breath. See if you can take ten full breaths. Counting this way helps your mind be less distracted.

Sam is now on his way to school. He doesn't know it yet, but today he will help two other children feel better by simply **noticing** their breathing.

He notices Lenny, who is also on his way to school.
"Wow," thinks Sam. "That's an impressive wheelie!"

Lenny is a little too confident and loses concentration. Before he knows it, he loses his balance. You can see what happens next!

Sam runs over to help Lenny, whose knee is badly scraped.
Lenny sees the blood, feels the stinging, and starts to panic.
"What if I have to go to the hospital?"

Luckily, Sam has some good advice to help Lenny calm down.

"Try not to worry about what might happen later. What really helps is to pay attention to your breathing. That will **relax** you, and when you relax you don't feel the pain as much."

Sam was right! After a minute or two of noticing his breathing, Lenny still feels the pain in his knee, but it's not as bad.

▶ PAUSE BUTTON

When was the last time you felt something painful? See if you can picture yourself in that situation. Now, see yourself breathing slow and deep breaths even while the pain is there. You can imagine that your breaths are friendly and smiley, just like Sam!

Later that day after school, Sam is attending concert rehearsal. He's playing guitar. Tonight the whole school will watch him.

This is Rosa. She's singing in the show. It's her first time onstage, and she's **nervous!** It's hard to rehearse when her head is filled with worries.

This looks like a job for . . . Super Sam! "I'm nervous too," he tells Rosa while they take a break. "But I can show you what helps me feel more **confident**."

Sam shows Rosa how to concentrate on her breathing, just like he showed Lenny. Rosa counts ten full breaths and begins to feel calmer.

"And now," says Sam, "see if you can notice how each breath feels. Is it rough? Smooth? Shallow or deep? Cool or warm?"

"Hmm," wonders Rosa.
"I've never noticed! Let me see . . ."

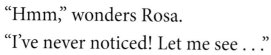 **PAUSE BUTTON**

Have you ever noticed how your breath feels? Take a moment now, close your eyes, and be curious. See if you can use three different words to describe what you notice.

There is no such thing as a right breath or a wrong breath. Every breath is different. You can never breathe the same breath twice!

Later that evening, Rosa is waiting to go onstage. There are so many people in the audience! Her tummy feels full of butterflies, but she is not worried.

The concert is a **success!** Sam and the band play well, Rosa hits her high notes, and the audience gives them a standing ovation.

"Bravo!" says the teacher, congratulating the children after the show.
"Well done, everyone. What a breath of fresh air that was!"

She doesn't realize how right she is! A breath of fresh air is always there to help us when we need it.

NOTES FOR PARENTS AND TEACHERS

Here are a few mindfulness exercises and breathing suggestions to add to children's Mindfulness Toolkits. These are simple, effective, and fun to do!

Balloon in the Belly

Breathing deeply into the belly (diaphragmatic breathing) supports a calm and relaxed body and mind. This practice helps children shift their breathing from the chest into the belly. (It's equally beneficial for adults!)

To really feel the effects of this type of breathing, lie down on a bed or the floor, close your eyes, and begin to notice your breathing. After a few breaths, place one hand on your chest and feel how far your hand moves as you breathe. Then, place your hand on your belly, and notice the amount of movement there. If there is more movement in the chest than in the belly, it tells you that you're not breathing deeply enough with the diaphragm.

You can encourage children to breathe more deeply by inviting them to imagine that there is a balloon in their belly that inflates when they breathe in and deflates when they breathe out. Ask children to choose a color for their balloon. Then invite them to close their eyes and imagine the balloon filling with the breath, then emptying. Children can keep their hands on the belly as they do this. If they become distracted by sounds or thoughts, they can simply notice the distraction and then choose to return their attention to the balloon.

A variation on this practice is to place a toy on the belly. Children can try to breathe smoothly and evenly so that the toy doesn't fall off.

7-11 Breathing

This practice is particularly helpful if children are feeling overwhelmed or anxious, or simply want to relax.

To use this technique, breathe in through the nose to the count of seven, pause, and then breathe out through the nose to the count of eleven. This ensures that the out-breath is longer than the in-breath, which enables the body's parasympathetic nervous system (PSN) to kick in. The PSN is responsible for calming the stress response in the body. Activating it when we feel stressed is an effective way to regulate physiological and emotional arousal.

You can also experiment with using shorter countdowns, such as breathing in to the count of five and out to the count of nine. Be careful not to rush the counting, though. Allow each breath enough space and time to reach its full length.

Breathe in the Good

In this exercise, children are encouraged to focus their attention on nourishing and affirming aspects of their lives.

First, ask them to call to mind something that makes them feel good, happy, or safe. Examples might be: a relationship with a close friend, family member, or pet; a place where they feel content and safe, such as in a bedroom, near a special tree, or at the beach; or something they feel grateful for—like the kindness of a grandparent, meals cooked by a parent, or the opportunity to learn how to play a musical instrument. Then, as they inhale, they imagine breathing in all the good feelings associated with this particular person (or animal), place, or object. Exhaling, they imagine breathing out these feelings and sharing them with the world so that everyone might benefit from this nourishing, positive energy.

Repeat this sequence a few times. Then invite children to notice how it feels to take in and give out such happy vibes!

BOOKS TO SHARE

Acorns to Great Oaks: Meditations for Children by Marie Delanote, illustrated by Jokanies (Findhorn Press, 2017)

Breathe and Be: A Book of Mindfulness Poems by Kate Coombs, illustrated by Anna Emilia Laitinen (Sounds True, 2017)

Breathe Like a Bear: 30 Mindful Moments for Kids to Feel Calm and Focused Anytime, Anywhere by Kira Willey, illustrated by Anni Betts (Rodale Kids, 2017)

I Am Peace: A Book of Mindfulness by Susan Verde, illustrated by Peter H. Reynolds (Abrams Books for Young Readers, 2017)

Sitting Still Like a Frog: Mindfulness Exercises for Kids (and Their Parents) by Eline Snel (Shambhala Publications, 2013)

Visiting Feelings by Lauren Rubenstein, illustrated by Shelly Hehenberger (Magination Press, 2014)

What Does It Mean to Be Present? by Rana DiOrio, illustrated by Eliza Wheeler (Little Pickle Stories, 2010)

A World of Pausabilities: An Exercise in Mindfulness by Frank J. Sileo, illustrated by Jennifer Zivoin (Magination Press, 2017)